DECEMBER **24**

'Twas the night before Christmas—
'TWAS PRACTICALLY HERE!
Every creature was ready
(and had been all year).

WHAT THE DINOSAURS
DID THE NIGHT BEFORE
CHRISTMAS

REFE & SUSAN TUMA

L B

Little, Brown and Company

**And now, after WEEKS
counting days 'til the date,
STILL there remained one last eve left to wait!**

So as I waited—tucked into my bed,
With visions of candy canes filling my head—

In my room,

where the clock

seemed to not move at all,

I decided I heard something out in the hall.

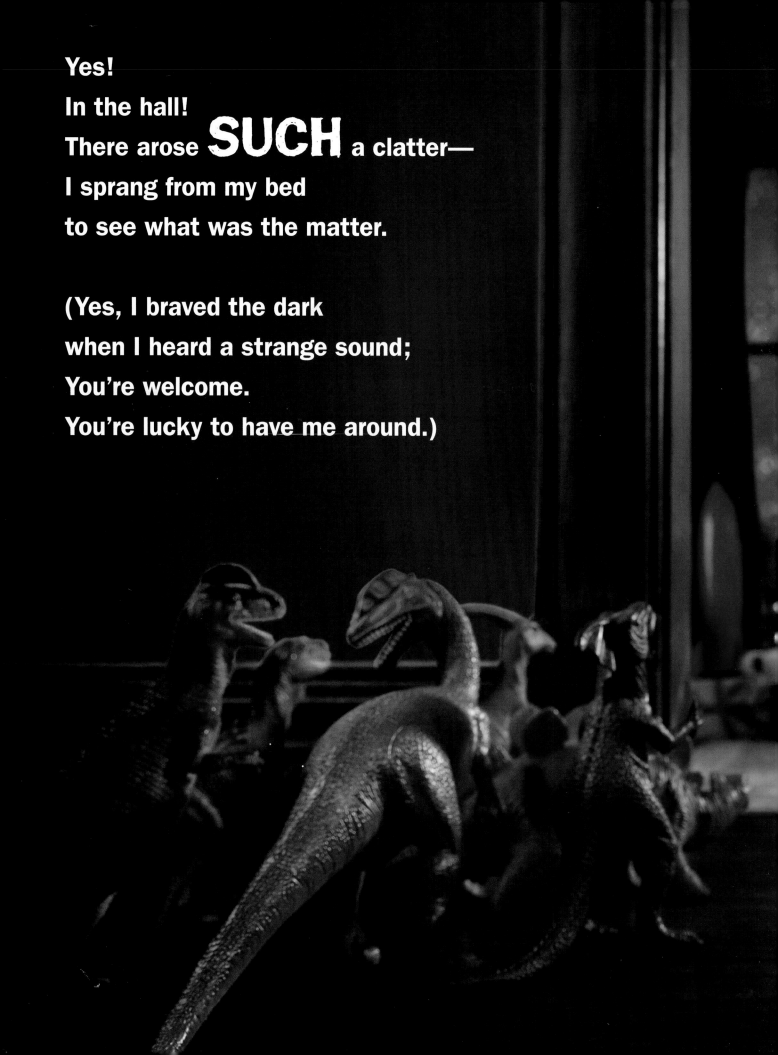

Yes!
In the hall!
There arose **SUCH** a clatter—
I sprang from my bed
to see what was the matter.

(Yes, I braved the dark
when I heard a strange sound;
You're welcome.
You're lucky to have me around.)

In the Christmas-Eve-moonlight-lit night,

Appeared, **BY ITSELF**,

such a marvelous sight:

Eight tiny dinosaurs, lively and quick...

...And one with a beard,

who **I KNEW** was Saint Nick.

They spoke not a word
but went straight to their work,
Their droll little smiles each turned in a smirk...

As they sampled the cookies,

inspected the lights...

And made sure the stockings

were hanging just right.

Then, finding the jar had been open since lunch,

**And added two floors to the gingerbread shack,
Very helpfully eating it when it collapsed.**

A brief note:

Before you pass judgment
on what happened next
(Which is something I doubt
you would EVER expect),
If you found, in YOUR hallway,
a dinosaur crew,
With a beard-wearing leader
you might have assumed
Was Saint Nicholas, coming to hurry along
The thing that you noticed
was taking too long—

REMEMBER:

I HAD WAITED A

VERY. LONG. TIME.

Then SANTA

(whose beard made

the claim it was he)

Climbed to straighten the star

at the top of the tree...

When it started
to **WIBBLE,**

and **WOBBLE,**

and **SWAY.**

So we scrambled
to quickly get out
of the way.

And while I'm not sure
what first caused me to doubt,
As the tree hit the ground
and the lights flickered out,

In the wake of the fall
I began to suspect
Maybe this wasn't Santa…

…and CHRISTMAS
was wrecked.

Then light from the just-risen
sun filled the room,
Saying, "Christmas is here!
You must clean this up—soon!"

I had waited for weeks.
Now I needed more time…

And Fake Santa was fleeing the scene of the crime!

He sprang to his sleigh,
to his team gave a whistle,
And lashed to the bottom
a little toy missile.

He shot out the chimney
and streaked cross the dawn...

In my sled, with my candy,
and then he was gone.

So I straightened the garland.

I righted the tree.

I reflected on how this could happen to me.

And the lesson
—for **ALL** of us—
seems crystal clear:

You can't trust a DINOSAUR wearing a BEARD.

WANTED:
FAKE SANTA CLAUS
not even real!
suspicious tail!
STOLEN
TOYS

For our parents

ABOUT THIS BOOK

This book was edited by Mary-Kate Gaudet and designed by Saho Fujii and Lynn El-Roeiy. The production was supervised by Bernadette Flinn, and the production editor was Jen Graham. The text was set in Franklin Gothic and Rachel Rabbits Lawn, and the display types are Rumble Brave and Lemon Yellow Sun.

The pictures in this book were taken on location using a Canon 6D DSLR camera. The dinosaurs, usually dormant outside the month of Dinovember, were animated for the duration of production using Christmas magic harvested from elves detained on charges of espionage, which was then reduced to a liquid concentrate and administered via eyedropper into the dinosaurs' daily feedings of butter tartare. Special thanks to Knotty Rug Co. of Kansas City for the use of one of their many beautiful rugs (we didn't even destroy it!), Lisa Keiler of the Baker E for the perfect holiday cookies (we *definitely* destroyed those...), Scott and Amanda Jolley for lenses, and pictureframes.com for rushing our order in the middle of a pandemic—the scenes in this book wouldn't be half as beautiful without each of you.

Copyright © 2021 by Refe Tuma and Susan Tuma • Cover illustration copyright © 2021 by Refe Tuma and Susan Tuma • Cover design by Saho Fujii and Lynn El-Roeiy • Cover copyright © 2021 by Hachette Book Group, Inc. • Hachette Book Group supports the right to free expression and the value of copyright. The purpose of copyright is to encourage writers and artists to produce the creative works that enrich our culture. • The scanning, uploading, and distribution of this book without permission is a theft of the author's intellectual property. If you would like permission to use material from the book (other than for review purposes), please contact permissions@hbgusa.com. Thank you for your support of the author's rights. • Little, Brown and Company • Hachette Book Group • 1290 Avenue of the Americas, New York, NY 10104 • Visit us at LBYR.com • First Edition: October 2021 • Little, Brown and Company is a division of Hachette Book Group, Inc. • The Little, Brown name and logo are trademarks of Hachette Book Group, Inc. • The publisher is not responsible for websites (or their content) that are not owned by the publisher. • Library of Congress Cataloging-in-Publication Data • Names: Tuma, Refe, author, illustrator. | Tuma, Susan, author, illustrator. • Title: What the dinosaurs did the night before Christmas / Refe & Susan Tuma. • Description: First edition. | New York : Little, Brown and Company, 2021. | Audience: Ages 4–8. | Summary: "In this reimagining of the classic ''Twas the Night Before Christmas,' the dinosaurs of Dinovember are up to all kinds of holiday mischief!" —Provided by publisher. • Identifiers: LCCN 2020032548 | ISBN 9780316539654 (hardcover) • Subjects: CYAC: Stories in rhyme. | Dinosaurs—Fiction. | Christmas—Fiction. | Behavior—Fiction. | Humorous stories. • Classification: LCC PZ8.3.T8255 Wh 2021 | DDC [E]—dc23 • LC record available at https://lccn.loc.gov/2020032548 • ISBN 978-0-316-53965-4 • PRINTED IN CHINA • APS • 10 9 8 7 6 5 4 3 2 1

Photo credits: Pages 1, 2, 5, 6, 8, 9, 10, 11, 12, 17, 21, 22, 27, 33, 34, 36 (masking tape) @ Michael Kraus/Shutterstock.com Page 5 (full moon in clouds) @ Mykola Mazuryk/Shutterstock.com • Pages 31–32 (pink sky) © Nature Style/Shutterstock.com